Also by Alison Claire Darke
The Nightingale

PUBLISHED BY DOUBLEDAY
a division of Bantam Doubleday Dell Publishing Group, Inc.
666 Fifth Avenue, New York, New York 10103

DOUBLEDAY
and the portrayal of an anchor with a dolphin
are trademarks of Doubleday, a division of
Bantam Doubleday Dell Publishing Group, Inc.

Library of Congress Cataloging-in-Publication Data
Andersen, H. C. (Hans Christian), 1805–1875,
[Tommelise, English]
Thumbelina/by Hans Christian Andersen; illustrated by Alison
Claire Darke.—1st ed. in the U.S.A.
p.   cm.
Translation of: Tommelise.
A tiny girl no bigger than a thumb is stolen by a great, ugly
toad, and subsequently has many adventures and makes many animal
friends before finding the perfect mate in a warm and beautiful
southern land.
[1. Fairy tales.] I. Darke, Alison Claire, ill. II. Title.
PZ8.A542Th   1990b
[E]—dc20 90-3664 CIP AC
ISBN 0-385-41403-X
0-385-41404-8 (lib. bdg.)
R.L. 3.3

PRINTED IN GREAT BRITAIN BY BPCC HAZELL BOOKS, PAULTON AND AYLESBURY
SEPTEMBER 1991
FIRST EDITION IN THE UNITED STATES OF AMERICA

E
And

Thumbelina

HANS CHRISTIAN ANDERSEN
ILLUSTRATED BY
ALISON CLAIRE DARKE

DOUBLEDAY
NEW YORK LONDON TORONTO SYDNEY AUCKLAND

Once there was a woman who was sad because she had no children. So one day she decided to go and seek help from a kind old witch.

"Why, yes," said the old witch. "That is easy to fix. Take this magic grain of barley and plant it in your garden. Soon you will have your wish."

The woman thanked her and returned home. She planted the grain carefully and sat back to wait. A moment later, to her surprise, a wonderful flower sprang up. It was beautiful, but its petals were tightly shut.

"What a pretty flower," said the woman, tenderly kissing its petals. And as she kissed it, the flower burst open.

The woman gasped. Sitting in the middle of the flower, smiling up at her, was a tiny little girl.

"Why, you're no bigger than my thumb," she said. "I'll call you Thumbelina."

The woman gave her little daughter a walnut shell for her bed and rose petals for her eiderdown.

During the day, Thumbelina loved to play. One of her favorite games was to float in a tulip-petal boat on a plate of water, and to row herself back and forth with two white horse hairs. She had a lovely voice, too, and enchanted the woman with her songs.

As she watched the tiny girl play and sing, the woman could not have been happier.

One night, however, as Thumbelina lay fast asleep in her walnut-shell bed, an ugly old toad came stealing in through the open window.

"What a dainty wife she would make for my son," she thought to herself. Quick as a flash, she snatched up the sleepy little girl, and hopped back through the garden to the muddy bank of the stream where she lived. Leaving Thumbelina stranded on a lily leaf, she hurried off to find her son.

In the morning, the old toad brought her son to see the tiny girl. "Ugh!" thought Thumbelina. She had never seen such an ugly, slimy creature. She shrank back as the young toad bounded toward her.

He gazed at her lovingly, but "Croak, croak, croooak!" was all he could say.

"Good," said his mother. "That seems settled, then." And she dragged her son away to prepare a home in the muddy bank for his little bride-to-be.

Thumbelina sat quite alone on the big green lily leaf surrounded by deep, green water, and she wept.

"Oh, if only I didn't have to marry that horrid, ugly toad!" she cried.

Down in the water the fishes heard Thumbelina's sobbing and felt sorry for the little girl. They were determined to set her free. Quickly, they gnawed through the lily leaf's stalk and Thumbelina floated slowly down the stream. She only hoped she would be far enough away before the toads returned.

Shortly, a pretty white butterfly fluttered down and settled on the leaf. "I can help you," he said eagerly. "Tie your sash around my waist and we'll speed along faster than the wind."

Together they glided swiftly past hills and meadows and trees until they entered a new land.

Thumbelina thought she was safe at last.

But all of a sudden a great beetle buzzed over her head. He saw the curious little girl and thought she was the prettiest thing he'd ever set eyes on. In a flash he swooped down, fastened his claws around her and swept her up into his tree.

Thumbelina was terrified, but the beetle didn't care. He was proud of his catch and called his sisters over to see. They were not impressed.

"What a strange, ugly creature," sneered one.

"Ha, ha! She's only got two legs," laughed another.

"Oh! How terribly thin she is. And look, my dears, she has no antennae!"

The beetle didn't like being laughed at. He decided to get rid of Thumbelina, and set her down on a daisy beneath his tree.

Now she was all alone in the forest.

But Thumbelina refused to be downhearted. She found berries to eat, drank nectar from the flowers and dew from the leaves. When evening came, she braided some grass to make a hammock, hung it between two leaves and slept peacefully.

Throughout the summer and autumn she lived happily in the forest. But when the long cold winter drew near, the birds who had sung to her flew away. The leaves fell from the trees, and the flowers shriveled and died. Gradually, even the little animals she had befriended left her. Before long, the frosts came and it began to snow.

Thumbelina wrapped herself in a withered leaf and decided she, too, must search for shelter. She stumbled through the forest, shivering with cold. Each snowflake that fell nearly buried the tiny girl, and the icy wind stung her face and hands.

At last she reached the edge of the forest and peered into the cornfield beyond. In the hedgerow, half buried in the snow, she found a small door. She barely had the strength to knock before she collapsed in the snow, completely exhausted.

There was a scurrying noise and the door opened. A field mouse appeared in the doorway, and her eyes opened wide with surprise when she saw the girl lying there. "Oh, you poor little thing," she cried. "Come inside quickly and get warm."

As Thumbelina sat by the fire in the field mouse's cozy home, she began to recover. She explained how she came to be wandering all alone in the forest, and the kind field mouse would not hear of her going out into the cold again.

"No," she insisted, "you must spend the winter here with me where you'll be safe and warm.

"Besides," she continued, "my neighbor, the mole, is coming to visit. He is a very well-to-do old gentleman. He has a most magnificent house and wears a fine black velvet jacket. It would entertain him so much if you would sing for him."

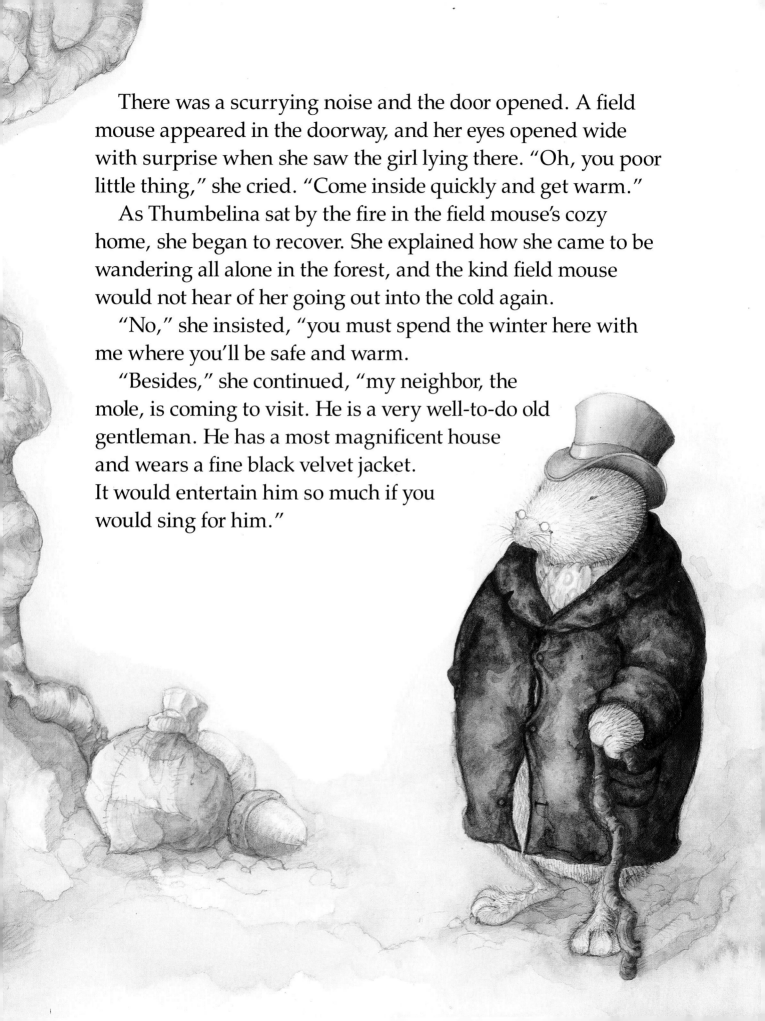

But Thumbelina didn't like the old mole. He scorned the sun and the flowers she loved so much, and she found him dull. Dutifully she sang for him, however. Indeed, she sang so sweetly that the mole soon fell in love with her. He started to visit them every day for tea and finally invited them to visit his home.

The three of them walked along the dark passageway that he had tunneled between their houses. At one point the mole stopped and exclaimed, "Oh! How disgraceful. There is a dead bird lying in the way." It was a poor swallow who had hurt his wing and so hadn't managed to fly with the other birds to warmer lands for the winter. But the mole didn't care. "Stupid creatures, birds," he grunted, kicking it aside. "All he could do was sing, and look where that got him."

The field mouse tut-tutted in agreement, but Thumbelina remembered her friends from the summer. She knelt by the bird, stroked his feathers and kissed his closed eyes.

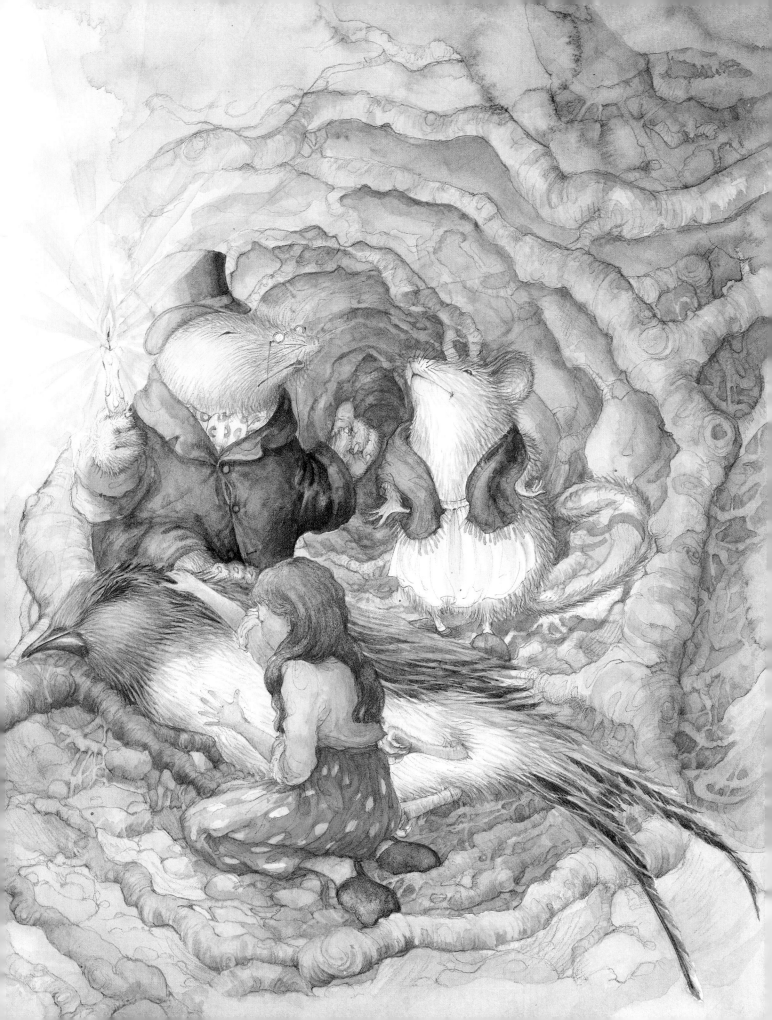

That night Thumbelina felt such an aching sorrow for the swallow that she couldn't sleep. So she took a blanket and crept back to the tunnel. Covering the bird, she laid her head on his chest.

She sprang back in shock. She could hear the faint beat of his heart. "Oh!" she cried. "You're not dead after all. But, poor swallow, you're so terribly weak. I shall look after you and make you well again."

And so, secretly, she visited the swallow every night to give him food and water. Through the winter the swallow slowly grew stronger. On the first day of summer he was well enough to fly away. "Come with me, little friend," the swallow begged her.

"I cannot," said Thumbelina. "The field mouse has been so kind to me, I couldn't think of leaving her."

So they said farewell and Thumbelina sadly waved goodbye as the swallow flew off into the forest.

It was decided that Thumbelina should be married to the mole at the end of the summer and that she would go and live with him in his magnificent underground home.

"What a piece of fortune," said the field mouse. "Such a fine and handsome husband. We must spend the summer preparing some clothes suitable for the wife of such a well-respected gentleman. I will ask some spiders to come and help us spin the cloth."

Thumbelina worked so hard she saw nothing of the summer sun. Now it was autumn and the day of the wedding approached. Soon her new life with the mole would begin and all her days would be spent underground.

"But I might never see or feel the sun again," she wept.

"Don't be so silly," snapped the field mouse. "Think of all the wealth and finery you will have."

But Thumbelina was still unhappy. "I must go and see the sun for the last time," she thought. She crept outside and stretched up her arms to feel its warmth. "How I wish I had gone with the swallow," she cried.

At that moment she heard a flutter of wings. She looked up and saw her friend flying overhead. They were overjoyed to see each other again. Thumbelina told the swallow how unhappy she was. "I will never see the flowers and birds again," she sobbed. "What shall I do?"

"Fly away with me now, Thumbelina," the swallow urged her. "Leave the mole and his dark and dismal home behind. The winter is coming and I'm off to warmer lands. Come with me."

"Oh, yes! I will," cried Thumbelina. Without delay, she climbed onto the swallow's back and away they flew.

High up in the sky they soared, on and on until finally the swallow settled on the ruins of a white palace.

"This is my home," he said. "Now you may choose one of these flowers to live in."

Thumbelina pointed to a beautiful white flower and the bird set her down on its soft petals.

There, to her amazement, sat a handsome prince, as tiny as she. He had the finest pair of butterfly wings and wore a golden crown. He smiled at Thumbelina and gently placed his crown upon her head. "Will you be my bride and Queen of all the flower spirits?" he asked.

Thumbelina gazed back at the Prince. "How wonderful," she said. "Yes, I will be your bride." The Prince was overjoyed and he gave Thumbelina a delicate pair of wings so that she, too, could fly from flower to flower. From all the flowers around came the other flower spirits bringing gifts to their new queen.

The swallow's heart was glad that Thumbelina had at last found happiness. From that day on, wherever he flew, he would sing his song about his dear little friend, and that is how we know the tale today.